BE D.O.P.E.

Be Dependent on Prayer Every Day

Jessica Carol-lyn

Publisher: Elite Publications

First Printing: April 24, 2020

Language: English

ISBN-13: 979-8636642626

www.elitepublications.org

Ordering Information: Special discounts are available on quantity purchases by corporations, associations, educators, and others. For details, contact the publisher at info@elitepublications.org.

U.S. trade bookstores and wholesalers: Please contact Jessie Bowen at (919) 618-8075 or email info@elitepublications.org.

Dedication

This book is dedicated to my loving parents, Leon A. Phillips, Sr. and Iris M. Phillips who taught me how to pray, the power of prayer, supported my endeavors, and told me that I can do all things through Christ. I know that you both are smiling from heaven. I love you!

Thank You

Jessie and Gwen Bowen (Pops and Mama), I can't thank you enough for the direction, wisdom, and love you you give me. You both push and stretch me to be the best version of Jessica that I can be. I am forever grateful God placed you both in my life. I love you, Pops and Mama! "I want to be like you when I grow up."

Leon A. Phillips, Jr., you are my brother and best friend. Thank you for always being in my corner, supportive, and prayerful. I love you!

Iyesha "Joy" Phillips, my best friend and sister, thank you. You know all of me, yet still love me. Thank you for bringing joy to my life. I love you!

Karissa Denae Johnson, my amazing friend and sister, I can not thank you enough. You are an inspiration. You encourage and motivate me to move fearlessly in the direction of my dreams. I love you!

Lastly, thank you to my wonderful support system. You all truly make me better and I am blessed to have you in my life. I love you!

Table of Contents

Foreword

By Karissa Denae Johnson

If we're honest with ourselves, we often leave prayer as a last resort. We scramble to pray when in distress. We reach for it in times of desperation. And sometimes we simply forget to pray altogether. Thankfully, regardless of when we pray or how we prioritize prayer, God hears us. Our gracious Father hears our prayers, whether we're wailing or whispering. He hears us when our prayers are planned or in panic mode. God finds joy in fellowshipping with us--period. He simply wants us to come.

God invites us to build a relationship with Him each and every day. Daily prayer strengthens our relationship with God and intensifies His voice. Depending on prayer every day will enhance every area of our lives. When we seek God, we seek His will. His will is for us to prosper and be in health, even as our souls prosper.

BE D. O. P. E. invites you to explore God's love, grace, and mercy on a deeper level. This book will usher you into intimate fellowship with the Father and guide you on how to work well with the people He's placed in your life.

When you apply the timeless tools in the pages to come, you will forever be dope.

A Letter to the Reader

Whether you are a child, preteen, teen, or adult, this book was created with you in mind. This was designed to help draw you closer to God, and to help you to walk with Christ as He leads. In this devotional, you will hear me guide you through my personal journey, what I learned, what I could have done differently, and how I developed an ear to hear the voice of God.

I want to take you on the journey because I feel that how I applied the Word of God isn't a way that's just for me, but you can use the same pattern as well. As I lead, you will apply the Word to your life and see magnificent changes that can only take place through Christ. You will begin to hear God more clearly. You will see His hand on your life in unique and fascinating ways. And your relationship will grow like never before.

I don't want you to imitate me; I want you to imitate Christ. We all have to learn who Jesus is for ourselves. I just want to help jumpstart or fine-tune your walk with him.

Brace yourselves. It's going to be one transparent, honest, open, and humbling ride--but it will all be worth it!

Remember, I am rooting for you!

Jessica Carol-lyn

Day 1: What's in Your Heart to Do?

"Take delight in the Lord, and He will give you the desires of your heart." (Psalm 37:4 NIV)

Have you ever thought about what you wanted to do in life? You've probably imagined when or what age you want to have it completed. Perhaps you thought about where you want to travel. Maybe you thought about marriage. Maybe you thought about owning a business. Maybe you thought about going to college. Or maybe you thought about purchasing a home or getting your own place. Whatever you might want to do in life, it's important that you run it by God and obtain a plan so He can help you through it. You want to make sure that His guidance and leadership are with you.

Let's look up the meaning of desire:

de·sire

noun

a strong feeling of wanting to have something or wishing for something to happen.

"a desire to work in the dirt with your bare hands."

verb

strongly wish for or want (something).

"He never achieved the status he so desired."

Now that we have the meaning of desire, think about yours. What are your desires? Choose five and write them below.

1.

2.

3.

4.

5.

Now let's think about your list above for a moment. How many of these have you prayed about? How many have you taken to God and submitted them to Him to see if this is the right moment for you to set out towards these desires?

Think about that then continue to read.

I remember moving from New York to a new city--a very unfamiliar place. I didn't know anyone besides my Dad and younger brother. I moved in with my dad for a while before moving in with a good friend after some time. Soon enough, my life shifted and I could no longer stay in the apartment. I began to seek God. I prayed and I prayed for a place to call my own. This prayer was prayed for years--5 years to be exact.

You see, God didn't open the door for my own place because it wasn't the season for me to have my own place. And although I prayed and it was my desire, it didn't align with His will. He didn't open that door until HE was ready to release it to me.

I can give you many examples of when I desired something, but God held it off. I invite you to write down which of your desires align with God's desires for your life.

If you find that some aren't in His will for your life, don't worry. You are not alone. The great part about it is that God always has something greater than we could even imagine or think lined up for our lives. We just need to walk in obedience *and have faith and patience. He absolutely knows what's best for our lives.*

Which of your desires matches God's? Write them below.

1.

2.

3.

4.

5.

How many of your desires matched God's? How many did not match? Either way, I believe it is time to pray and ask God for guidance. Even if you have prayed before, there may be something that

God wants you to see or hear in particular. When you pray, ask Him to release you from your will and attach you to His. When you pray, allow Him to align your will with His will.

Put aside your idea of how your life should be. Trust me, I know how hard or uncomfortable this may be at times. We have our dreams and aspirations. We have goals and there's nothing wrong with having those things. We just want to make sure that our dreams come underneath what God has for us to do. We want to make sure we are living faithfully, obediently, purposefully, and righteously. Living like this will automatically put you in the center of God's will. Clear your heart of your will and pray that God guides you through your list of desires.

Let's pray.

Dear Heavenly Father,

Thank you, Lord for opening my heart to Your will. I submit my plans to You. I want to live with Your desires at the forefront of my mind. Please help me to achieve the things that You want me to do. Open the doors to the opportunities that You want me to take. I trust You with my life and know that You will allow all things to work for my good. I not only need Your guidance--I want it--I DESIRE it. Please help me through life as I obey and travel in the direction of Your will. Consume my daily routine and eliminate anything that will stop me from moving forward in my purpose. I love You, Jesus. Amen.

Day 2: What Does Obedience Look Like For Me?

"Blessed are all who fear the Lord, who walk in obedience to Him." (Psalm 128:1 NIV)

Obedience is a word that we don't use too often. Sometimes it's because we have a problem being told what to do. Other times we may feel like we are being dominated. Or maybe it's because we are so caught up in our plans that we don't have time to stop and think about what God wants. Could it be that we are fearful of what God will ask us to do? Whatever it is, please know that obedience is a part of our Christian walk.

Obedience looks different season to season and person to person. Whatever it may look like, we are guaranteed to cross paths with it. It may look like spending less money for me and applying to a

17

certain school for you. I may need to stop hanging out with a certain group of people and you may need to spend less time on social media. I may need to take a lower salary job and you may need to move across the country to accept a position at a job in a town where you don't know anyone. It just depends on what God is asking of you and your life. One thing is for sure: as we walk with Christ, obedience is necessary. It's required in order for us to grow in Christ and see His wonderful and glorious fruit in our lives.

Do you know that obedience is a sign of surrendering? What are we surrendering? Our will, life plans, finances, heart, time--the list goes on and on. To sum it up: we surrender our lives. Yes, our lives. I know that may be a bit overwhelming for some, but trust me, the more you walk in it, the easier it becomes. You see, God wants us to walk in complete obedience to His

Word. But how do you know when you are walking in obedience? Here's a small checklist to help you determine if you are walking in obedience or if you need to adjust your habits to His.

- You <u>read</u> your Bible daily.

- You <u>pray</u> daily.

- You care more about <u>His desires</u> more than your own.

- You <u>seek</u> His direction.

- You <u>listen</u> to His voice and <u>respond</u> with "Yes, Lord."

Take a moment to go back to the list above.

Read it again.

Don't rush through it, but take it in. Take your time.

How did you respond to this list? Are these things that you already do? Can you become more efficient in them? Can you grow a little more in an area?

Go back to the list and read again, but this time commit to doing one thing on the list for a day. That's right, just one day. I don't want you to become overwhelmed with the process.

Go back and read.

So, what did you commit to? Write it below:

_____

_____

Again, don't become overwhelmed with your decision. I want you to take your time and grow into it. Start today, then when tomorrow comes, do it again. When the next day comes, do it again. Before you know it, you will have completed a week, two weeks, three weeks, a month, and a year!

Let's go over some ways to help you stay on track:

1. **Keep a journal.** Keeping record of how you feel, what you've done, and how you progress will be a great way to track your growth.
2. **Choose an accountability partner.** Your partner will help to keep you motivated and cheer for you along the way.
3. **Set a reminder on your phone.** This is my personal favorite. I remember really wanting God to be the last person that I spoke to, but was having a hard time remembering to pray before I went to sleep. So, I set a reminder close to my bedtime. Before I knew it, I no longer needed the reminder because praying became part of me.

Just like these three things helped me stay committed to God and growing in obedience, I am sure they will help you to stay focused and committed to growth.

One last thing, read the title of this chapter and answer it below:

_____

_____

_____

_____

_____

_____

_____

_____

_____

_____

_____

_____

Let's pray.

Dear Heavenly Father,

Thank you for another opportunity to draw nearer to You, Jesus. Thank you for helping me to hear Your voice. Lord, please help me to always respond to Your voice with obedience. I want to do Your will. I just need help actually applying what You said to my life. I do love You and I am sure that You know that. Please help me to obey You even when I don't want to or when it's hard. Help me to look to You in all that I do. I want to be a better listener. I want to be a better person. I want to be a better Christian. I want to be OBEDIENT. Help me to be all of this and more. In Jesus' Name I pray, Amen.

Day 3: How Can You Be More Dependent on God?

"So do not fear, for I am with you; do not be dismayed, for I am your God. I will strengthen you and help you; I will uphold you with my righteous hand." (Isaiah 41:10 NIV)

Depending on someone can be a tough thing to do. Trust me, I totally get it. But unlike your friends, neighbor, family, or anyone else, God will not fail you. This is the best part about depending on God: His faithfulness.

Have you heard of the trust fall? It's when someone stands behind you and you fall expecting them to catch you. I've played this game several times. Sometimes I just fall and other times I can't muster enough trust in the person to blindly fall. I end up looking over my shoulder to make sure they are in position to catch me.

As you can see, just like this game, dependency involves trust. It partners with faith to help you believe in the person who is claiming to have your back. In this case, we are talking about God. No matter what, we must believe that God has our back. He wants you to be completely faithful that He will catch you every time. We can trust that He will be there every moment of our lives. When we need help with finances, He's there. When we need help choosing which job to take, He's there. When we lose our job, He's there. When we are a bit moody, He's there. When we are trying to get along with a person who is everything but nice, He's there.

You see, there isn't a moment that God isn't there to see us through whatever the situation is. It's up to us to believe and trust that God never leaves us (Deuteronomy 31:6).

Do you always count on Him to show up for you every time that you need Him?

We can have total dependence on God because, if you think about it, He's never let us down before. When we put our trust in the things that we have, like our job or people around us, it takes the glory from God. We shift our dependence from God to our bank account, car, job, best friend, and even ourselves. But depending on these things isn't the way to go. We weren't created to be dependent on ourselves and things; we were created to depend on God. He wants us to look to Him and trust that He will work all things together for our good (Romans 8:28).

So I encourage you to not look over your shoulder like I did in the trust fall, because God is always in position. He isn't going anywhere. Trust that God will always come through for you and your needs.

Jot down some areas of your life where you feel you can be more dependent and trusting in God.

_____

_____

_____

_____

_____

_____

_____

_____

_____

_____

_____

_____

_____

_____

_____

_____

_____

_____

_____

Let's Pray.

I invite you to pray. Write down your prayer below.

_____

_____

_____

_____

_____

_____

_____

_____

_____

_____

_____

_____

_____

_____

_____

_____

_____

Now take a moment to sit quietly and listen. What is God saying to you?

_____

_____

_____

_____

_____

My Encouragement Corner

"Death and life are in the power of the tongue, and those who love it and indulge it will eat its fruit and bear the consequences of their words." (Proverbs 18:21 AMP)

With so much going on in our current events, we could all use a little more encouragement. We sometimes look to others to give us an encouraging word, but I want you to take this time to build yourself up. Why? Because your words have life in them. We decide what comes out of our mouths. Make a conscious effort to bring beauty into your world by using the Word of God. I want you to use this page to encourage yourself and talk yourself into a better and healthier life and mindset. So as you write, speak out loud. After you finish writing, go to the mirror and speak to yourself.

God is listening and catching every word that comes from your mouth. Speak life, healing, and greatness into your health, finances, family, job, relationships, and other areas. READY? SET. GO!

_____

_____

_____

_____

_____

_____

_____

_____

_____

_____

_____

_____

Day 4: Faith: When Nothing Is Adding up

"By faith we understand that the universe was formed at God's command so that what is seen was not made out of what was visible." (Hebrews 11:3 NIV)

Faith can be scary and cause some people to panic when they are walking into the unknown with no idea of how anything is going to work out. When God asks us to do something, He wants our response to be one of obedience, sacrifice, and faith. But how many of us respond with obedience, sacrifice, and faith when things look like they don't make sense or don't add up? We live in a time when our faith is being tested daily. However, God is able to step into our lives and work a miracle in uncertain times. He will make something happen out of what we thought was nothing. How? Well, the only response I can give you is that God is powerful and almighty. He is God!

When we decide to do what God is asking of us, it allows God to show up for us and our family.

Responding to life's situations with faith lets God know that you are open to Him moving powerfully in your life. You are giving Him access to your life and when He has access, only one thing can happen: miracles. Whether you need a miracle in your marriage, school, job, finances, health, or something else, faith will put you on Miracle Boulevard. It will set your life up to see the goodness and glory of God.

Please know, "Faith doesn't make things easy, it makes things possible."

Right now I want you to think about what areas in your faith have been shaken or tested. What has God asked you to do that you just can't seem to move forward on? What is going on in your life

that is causing you to step your faith game up?
Use the space below to jot down your thoughts.

_____

_____

_____

_____

_____

_____

_____

_____

_____

_____

_____

_____

_____

_____

_____

_____

_____

_____

_____

_____

_____

Now, let's feed your faith with the Word of God. Study the scriptures below to help you move past whatever is holding you back from moving forward in faith. As you study, apply each scripture to your life and ask God to help you trust Him and listen to Him during this time.

1.   *"He replied, because you have so little faith. Truly I tell you, if you have faith as small as a mustard seed, you can say to this mountain, move from here to there, and it will move. Nothing will be impossible for you." Matthew 17:20 NIV*

2.   *"And we know that in all things God works for the good of those who love Him, who have been called according to His purpose." Romans 8:28 NIV*

3.   *"Early in the morning, as Jesus was on His way to the city, He was hungry. Seeing a fig tree by the road, He went up to eat but found nothing on it except leaves. Then He said to it, "May you never bear fruit again!" Immediately the tree withered. When the disciples saw this, they were amazed. "How did the fig tree wither so quickly?" they asked. Jesus replied, "Truly I tell you, if you have faith and do not doubt, not only can you do what was done to the fig tree, but also you can say to this mountain, 'Go throw yourself into the sea,' and it will be done. If you believe, you will receive whatever you ask for in prayer." Matthew 21:18-22 NIV*

Remember, when we trust God completely and totally with our lives, He is now able to do exceeding abundantly above all we can ask or think according to the power that works in us (Ephesians 3:20). What is stopping you from submitting to Him and trusting that God will do it? Unlock the unexpected, impossible, and unbelievable by giving

God your faith. So, what's possible when we give God faith? Everything!

Let's Pray.

Dear Heavenly Father,

I give you glory and praise for positioning me so strategically in life. There is nothing that I am going through that You don't know about. My faith needs help. I need a boost. Help me to trust you more. Help me to read Your Word more. Help me to turn away from fear and walk boldly in the things of You. As You lead, I want to follow. I trust in You. In Jesus' Name, Amen.

Day 5: God's Strength & Peace

"The Lord will give strength unto His people; the Lord will bless His people with peace." (Psalm 29:11 KJV)

Step One: *Read today's scripture.*

Step Two: *Jot down your thoughts pertaining to the scripture below.*

_____

_____

_____

_____

_____

_____

_____

_____

_____

_____

_____

_____

_____

_____

Step Three: *Read today's devotion.*

Where are you today? What are you holding on to? No, I am not talking about your phone, pen, or any tangible item. Spiritually speaking, what are you holding on to?

Today is a new day. It's full of new blessings, grace, mercy, adventures, and mindsets. Well, at least it should be all of these things and more. Unfortunately, we seem to hold on to things that happened yesterday, last week, or even things that happened last year. And holding on to these things impacts how we respond to life today. This is why one word can trigger a bad memory. We hold on to the not-so-kind words that someone spoke to us. We hold on to doubt and fear. We hold on to getting let go from a job. We even hold on to not being accepted into a school or a certain social club. But we need to learn how to let these things go and God is here to help us with this.

Pause for a moment and read today's scripture again. As you read, think of those things or people you need strength letting go of and ask God for peace to help you do so. God doesn't want us to be held captive to yesterday's thoughts or previous situations. He wants us to trust that He will help us grow and heal from those things that happened to us in our childhood or adult years.

Letting go and trusting God isn't always easy. You have been carrying this burden for a while and it's become a part of you. But God wants healing to invade the broken areas of your life. He wants peace to fill the chaotic areas, and He wants His love to fill those voids. It takes strength to get through those tough times, but it also takes strength to let go.

Will you let go of what you are holding on to? God's hand is extended today; will you give what is in your hand to God? He will nurture you back to health and make you stronger in Him.

Reach for His hand.

Let's Pray.

Dear Heavenly Father,

You are asking me to let go of _____ and I need help letting go. I know that Your peace, strength, and love are needed with this transition. I want it all from You. Please give me a new way of thinking. Help me to feel better about myself. Help me to even resist the thoughts that try to come back to my mind. I am reaching for You with this prayer. I know there is more that You can give me if I release what I am holding on to. I will let go of it and rest knowing that You are King and Lord of my life. I extend my heart and all of the brokenness, anger, fear, and pain that has consumed me. I release my life to You. Help me overcome this. Thank You. In Jesus' Name, Amen.

Day 6: The Grace of God

"But He giveth more grace. Wherefore He saith, God resisteth the proud, but giveth grace unto the humble." (James 4:6 KJV)

The more I live, the more I experience the love of God that's offered to me through His grace. There are moments when I feel awful because I intentionally disobeyed God's instruction. What about you? Have you ever been told to do something by your parents and you didn't listen? You expected your parents to become angry. You just knew that they had enough. But what did they do after they cooled down? They showed you that although they were upset, they never stopped loving you. That is a demonstration of grace.

Yes, God does correct us. And even in correction, He never stops loving us. He's there to give us another chance. God knows that His children will need His grace, so He offers it to us freely.

Think for a moment. When was the last time you needed grace?

Let's think again. When was the last time you extended grace to someone?

One more: When was the last time you extended grace to yourself?

In life we are definitely going to have moments that absolutely call for the grace of God to cover us. But we must remember to extend that same grace to ourselves and others with the same measure He extends it to us. Don't hold people to their mistakes or even what they did to you on purpose.

Instead, pray and offer them grace and allow God to do the rest.

Let's pray.

Dear Heavenly Father,

Thank You for the grace that You willingly give to me every day. Thank You for covering my life with Your grace, mercy, and love. Help me to be aware of my actions towards You, others, and myself. Help me to love them better by showing them grace and in return they will see You through my actions. I want my life to give You glory. Help me to walk lovingly and graciously in this world. In Jesus' Name, Amen.

Day 7: What Now, God?

"Trust in the Lord with all your heart and lean not on your own understanding; in all your ways submit to Him, and He will make your paths straight."
Proverbs 3:5-6 (NIV)

Do you want to know what one of my favorite games is? Trouble. You know the game for up to four players? It has four colors with pegs that you move from start to finish. You push the round dome in the middle that has a die in it. Whatever number it lands on is the amount of spaces that you move your peg.

We can look at our lives through this game. Let's say that God is the die in the middle and we are the pegs moving. We should live our lives based on the steps that God has us take. If He says to go forward two steps, we should move two steps.

If He says move back four steps, we should automatically move back four steps. We may not always like the response that God gives us, but we can trust that it is the greatest direction we can get.

God expects us to listen to His direction daily. But the only way that we are going to hear Him speak is if we willingly listen. We should listen with obedience being our main goal. Our days are so consumed with our schedules, friends, work, eating, working out, etc. All God wants us to do is stop for a moment and consult Him. His direction is needed more than ever these days. His direction is full of wisdom, love, and protection.

When we ask God for His direction, we are setting ourselves up for greatness and guidance. We are genuinely asking God, "What do You think?" and "Which way should I go?"

List some things that you need direction in below:

1. _____

_____

_____

2. _____

_____

_____

3. _____

_____

_____

4. _____

_____

_____

5. _____

_____

_____

6. _____

_____

_____

7. _____

_____

8. _____

_____

9. _____

_____

_____

_____

Pray through this list and ask God to lead and direct your steps as you acknowledge His presence in your life.

Let's Pray.

Dear Heavenly Father,

Jesus, thank You for this day. I am coming to You for guidance. I acknowledge that You have all of the answers. Please help me figure out which road to take. I am at a crossroads and want to make the best decision for my life. Only You know what the future holds. So please guide me on this journey called life. Help me to move according to Your will and stay connected to You. In Jesus' Name, Amen.

About the Author

Jessica Carol-lyn is a minister, mentor, and author. She believes in the power of her words and only speaks greatness into her life and the lives of others.

As a child, Jessica loved Jesus. She grew up in church, but didn't desire to grow her relationship with Christ until later in life. Soon, she began to see herself through the eyes of Jesus. He began to develop her life spiritually, mentally, emotionally, and physically. Jessica went from being shy and quiet to outgoing and talkative. God's light began to shine through her.

Jessica desires everyone to know Christ on a deeper level. This shows through her debut book BE D.O.P.E.: Be Dependent on Prayer Every Day. The reader will feel encouraged, enlightened, and drawn to prayer after they've finished reading.

Jessica says, "There's something about the way my pen flows when God writes through me. I'm in love with His words and penmanship."

In her spare time, Jessica enjoys photography, outdoor excursions, adventurous activities and spending time with her family and friends. You'll also find that she enjoys sipping hot tea while watching a good movie.

Made in the USA
Las Vegas, NV
15 July 2021